THE TINIEST TUMBLEWEED

by **Kathy Peach**

Illustrated by **Alex Lopez**

Reading with Peaches, LLC
kpeach12@cox.net

*Previously published by Little Five Star,
a division of Five Star Publications, Inc.*

www.TiniestTumbleweed.com

Illustrator: Alex Lopez
Cover Design & Page Layout: Jeff Yesh
Editor: Conrad J. Storad
Curriculum Guide Contributors: Maki Wojcicki and Melinda Hutchison, M.Ed.
Proofreaders: Deb Greenberg and Ruthann Raitter
Project Manager: Patti Crane

Publisher's Cataloging-In-Publication Data

Peach, Kathy.
   The tiniest tumbleweed / by Kathy Peach ; illustrated by Alex Lopez.

     pages : color illustrations ; cm

   Summary: The tiniest tumbleweed is small for her age. So is her Sonoran Desert neighbor, a baby house sparrow. But both work within their limitations and learn to believe in themselves and their unique capabilities. Includes fun facts and curriculum guide.

   Interest age level: 005-009.
   Issued also as an ebook.
   ISBN: 978-0-9981033-0-3
   eISBN: 978-0-9981033-1-0

   1. Russian thistle--Growth--Juvenile fiction. 2. Sparrows--Growth--Juvenile fiction. 3. Ability--Juvenile fiction. 4. Self-actualization (Psychology)--Juvenile fiction. 5. Tumbleweeds--Growth--Fiction.
6. Sparrows--Growth--Fiction. 7. Ability--Fiction. 8. Self-actualization (Psychology)--Fiction. I. Lopez, Alex, 1971- II. Title.

PZ7.1.P433 Ti 2016
[E]   2015942668

Printed in the United States of America

10 9 8 7 6 5 4

DEDICATIONS

It is with sincere gratitude that I dedicate this book to Professor Sharon Fagan. Because of your devotion and contributions to the world of children's literature, my interest in producing a piece of quality literature was cultivated. Thank you for being the inspiration that awakened my dream of one day writing a children's book.

—Kathy Peach

To my wonderful wife, Lorraine, and precious daughters, Hannah, Haley, and Hazel. My art is not created solely by skill and talent, but is driven by their love and support.

—Alex Lopez

ACKNOWLEDGMENTS

*To Barrett, The Honors College at Arizona State University: Thank you for the opportunity and venue to make **The Tiniest Tumbleweed** a reality. Thank you, Ashley Yost and Dr. Wendy Oakes, for sharing the original vision.*

—Kathy Peach

"She's here," said Mother Tumbleweed with a big, warm smile. "Ohhh," said Father Tumbleweed. "She is so tiny."

"Yes," Mother Tumbleweed nodded. "She is the tiniest tumbleweed."

Father was concerned. What if she was too tiny to make seeds and provide rest for the sparrows like her brothers and sisters?

Mother Tumbleweed gently rocked her new baby. "She will grow. I am quite sure of it. I am quite sure, indeed."

Nearby a baby sparrow hatched.

"He is very small," said Father Sparrow.
He wondered if his new sparrow would grow to
fly and spread seeds like his brothers and sisters.

Mother Sparrow was not concerned.
"He will grow," she said, smiling at Baby Sparrow.

Over time, Tiny Tumbleweed did grow ... just not as much as her brothers and sisters. She became very sad.

And Baby Sparrow grew, too ... just not as much as his brothers and sisters. He, too, became very sad.

Mother and Father Tumbleweed loved Tiny Tumbleweed very much. They noticed her sadness.

"I am not growing like my brothers and sisters," said Tiny Tumbleweed. Mother Tumbleweed nodded and said, "Hmmm."

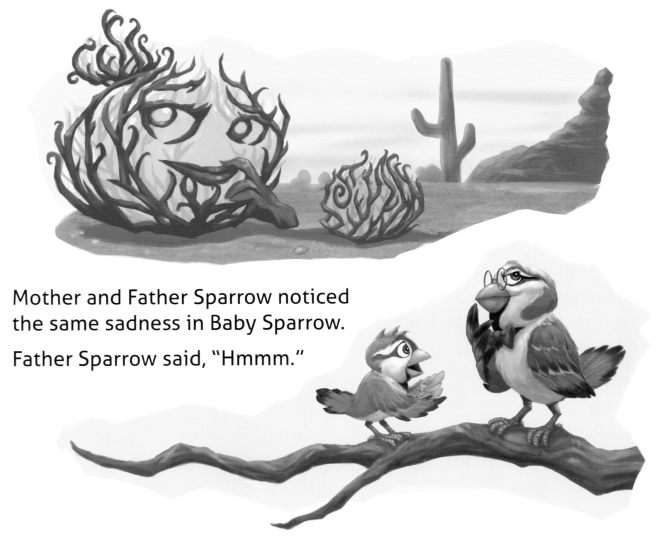

Mother and Father Sparrow noticed the same sadness in Baby Sparrow.

Father Sparrow said, "Hmmm."

Mother Tumbleweed thought and thought about how to help Tiny Tumbleweed.

One day she had a grand idea. She explained that the desert rains would soon come. Tiny Tumbleweed would be able to push her roots deep into the soil and take in good food. The food would help her grow strong and make beautiful flowers that would bloom and make seeds.

Tiny Tumbleweed was very thoughtful.
"Will I be as big and strong as my
brothers and sisters?"

"Perhaps not," said Mother. "But you will be as big and
strong as **YOU** can be and that is just fine, just fine indeed."
With that, she gave Tiny Tumbleweed a hug.

Father Sparrow knew just how to help Baby Sparrow.

"Baby Sparrow, sit here," he said in the voice fathers use when they are about to tell you things.

Baby Sparrow sat down on the ground and listened very carefully.

Father explained that wings become strong by stretching them open as far as possible and by flapping them up and down many, many times.

Baby Sparrow's eyes grew wide in amazement. His feathers ruffled from the wind Father made.

Next, Father hopped. "Hopping makes our legs strong so landing is easier." He hopped forward and then backward so Baby Sparrow would understand.

Baby Sparrow asked if he would be as big and strong as his brothers and sisters.

"Perhaps not," said Father. "But you will be as big and strong as **YOU** can be and that is just fine, just fine indeed." With that, he gave Baby Sparrow a hug.

Just as Mother Tumbleweed said, the desert rains came. Tiny Tumbleweed pushed her roots down into the softened soil. It was hard work.

She stretched out her branches over and over. Soon she was very tired.

"Keep trying," said her brothers and sisters.
"Your hard work will help you grow."

Slowly, she did begin to grow. Her stem became thicker.
Her branches became stronger. Her beautiful flowers bloomed,
making many seeds. She was a lovely Tiny Tumbleweed.

17

Baby Sparrow worked hard, too. He stretched and flapped and flapped and stretched. He hopped backward and forward. He wanted to grow and spread seeds like his brothers and sisters, so he kept at it, just like Father said.

He learned to fly.
He was becoming a
strong Young Sparrow.

One day, Young Sparrow decided to fly in a different direction to look for seeds. He flew and looked. He looked and flew. He did not, however, pay attention to the change in the color of the sky. Soon, the winds began to blow. Young Sparrow found it harder to fly.

"I must find shelter and a place to rest," he thought to himself. "And, I must *hurry* before the rain begins."

He flew faster toward a barn where cows were mooing. Then, he saw her—Tiny Tumbleweed. As he flew closer he could see that she was just the right size to provide shelter for him. Her stem looked strong. Her branches looked strong, too. Young Sparrow was very happy he had found such a wonderful Tiny Tumbleweed!

"Hello," he said. "May I sit in your branches until the rain is over?"

Tiny Tumbleweed smiled and stretched out her lowest branch. "Yes, of course. Hop up on my branch. You will be safe from the wind and rain." Young Sparrow hopped onto the branch. His small feet fit perfectly.

As the wind blew, Young Sparrow noticed Tiny Tumbleweed's seeds falling to the ground. "You have seeds—tiny seeds—seeds that are just the right size for my beak," he said.

"Will my seeds help you?" she asked.

"Oh, yes," said Young Sparrow. "I have searched for seeds such as these. I can gather and spread them, just like other sparrows."

Young Sparrow was glad he had stretched and flapped and hopped. The hard work had made his body strong. He could fly and spread seeds. He had become the sparrow he was created to be. He was a very happy sparrow, a very happy sparrow indeed.

Tiny Tumbleweed smiled a big smile. By making seeds and providing a place for a bird to rest, she had become the tumbleweed she was created to be. She was a very happy tumbleweed, a very happy tumbleweed indeed.

FUN FACTS

Tumbleweeds

- Tumbleweeds grow from tiny seeds. The seeds are so small that hundreds of them could fit in the palm of your hand.

- The seeds fall to ground from the host plant or are carried and dropped by birds. The wind also helps move seeds from one place to another.

- New plants form from seeds that take root. When the plants break through the ground, they begin as a single "shoot," the original stem. From the stem of each plant, several small branches with tiny green leaves develop. The branches grow quickly and form other branches. Initially, the new plants' color is dull mint green.

- As the plants grow, the branch stems become bright pink. The stems have red veins. Soon, flowers form and bloom, producing more seeds. The flowers are pale yellow with red centers.

- Mature tumbleweed plants can be quite large. They are round and dull, olive green.

- Eventually, the plants die and uproot from the ground. Then they are free to "tumble" in the wind.

House Sparrows

- House sparrows are small birds. They are often found living near people. The male is beautifully marked and looks as if he is wearing a black bandana.

- The female is a lovely bird, too. She has a longer, sleeker body than the male, and is not as colorful.

- House sparrows are fun to watch. When they move on the ground, they "hop" forward and backward rather than walk like other birds. They also have a loud call for a bird so small.

- Sparrows fly inside uprooted tumbleweeds and sit. Sometimes there are many, many sparrows sitting inside a single tumbleweed.

CURRICULUM GUIDE

This curriculum guide is designed to support Arizona's College and Career Ready Standards for English Language Arts, Third Grade. Depending on the student, the guide may be used to support second graders who are reading on an advanced level or fourth graders who need extra scaffolding.

Following are lists of discussion/writing prompts for reading/journaling utilizing a close read:

Key Ideas and Details from the Story

Discussion/writing prompts for reading/journaling using key ideas and details from the story:

1. How are Tiny Tumbleweed and Baby Sparrow different from their brothers and sisters? How do you know? Cite your evidence from the text.

2. How do you know that Tiny Tumbleweed's and Baby Sparrow's mothers were confident their babies would grow? Cite your evidence and page numbers from the text.

3. What idea did Mother Tumbleweed have to help Tiny Tumbleweed? Sentence starter: On page 10, the author said...

4. What did Father Sparrow suggest that Baby Sparrow do to help himself grow? Cite your evidence from the text.

5. List, in sequence, the actions Tiny Tumbleweed took to help herself grow. Identify the page number and support your answer from the text.

6. How did Tiny Tumbleweed's brothers and sisters help her? Support your answer from the text.

7. How did Tiny Tumbleweed help the sparrow? How did the sparrow help Tiny Tumbleweed? Support your answers from the text.

8. What was Baby Sparrow's motivation to do the hard work so he could grow? Cite your evidence from the text.

9. How did Young Sparrow feel about his accomplishment after his hard work? How do you know? Support your evidence from the text.

10. Describe how Tiny Tumbleweed felt at the end of the story. Explain your answer.

11. Describe the relationship between Tiny Tumbleweed and Young Sparrow at the end of the story. Support your evidence from the story.

Craft and Structure

Discussion/writing prompts for reading/journaling using the illustrations and the structure of the book:

1. From what point of view is the story written? How do you know?

2. Describe the setting of the story. How do you know?

3. How did the author use illustrations to engage you in the events of the story?

4. How does the illustration on page 14 portray Father Sparrow's feelings about showing Baby Sparrow how to fly and how to hop?

5. How does the illustration on page 16 help you to know that Tiny Tumbleweed was working hard to help herself grow?

6. In the story, what happened to Tiny Tumbleweed also happens to Baby Sparrow. Why do you think the author wrote the story that way?

7. Why did the author write, "Baby Sparrow's eyes grew wide in amazement?"

8. Why did the author capitalize the word YOU on pages 11 and 15?

Integration of Knowledge and Ideas

Discussion/writing prompts for reading/journaling, integrating knowledge and ideas from the story:

1. What is the main idea or theme of the story?

2. How does the story connect to the theme of the book?

3. Do you agree with the author's position on the theme of the book? Why or why not?

4. What are your dreams and how will you help yourself achieve them?

5. Compare the similarities between the tumbleweed and sparrow families.

6. Think about another story where the characters had to work hard to overcome a problem. How is that story the same as or different from *The Tiniest Tumbleweed*?

7. What do you think was the author's purpose for writing this book?

Range of Reading and Level of Text Complexity

Discussion/writing prompt for reading/journaling, range of reading and level of text complexity from the story:

1. Think of a time in your life when you felt a sense of accomplishment after having worked hard to achieve a goal.

Research Project–Use of Technology

After reading, discussing, and writing about *The Tiniest Tumbleweed*, assign a research project to further students' knowledge of the Sonoran Desert. Below are suggested topics:

- Tumbleweeds
- House sparrows
- Sonoran Desert
- Sonoran Desert storms
- Desert animals

Bulletin Board Ideas

Download a FREE illustration of Tiny Tumbleweed at www.TiniestTumbleweed.com. Here is a suggestion for a bulletin board design using the illustration:

- Photograph each child and print the pictures.

- Using the tumbleweed illustration, affix the child's picture in the center.

- Create a simple desert scene as the bulletin board background. Use brown poster paper as the ground and blue poster paper for the sky. Draw a large Saguaro or several desert plants of choice.

- Display the student "tumbleweeds" randomly around the bulletin board in different positions—some sideways, some upright, and some almost upside down.

Suggested Bulletin Board Titles:

- *Tumbling into Kindergarten*
- *Tumbling out of Kindergarten into First Grade*
- *Look Who's Tumbling into Second Grade*
- *Look Who's Tumbling into Third Grade*

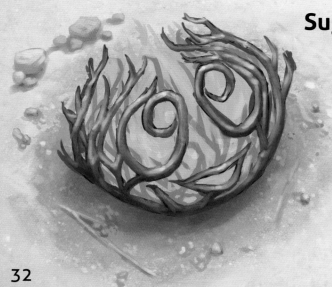

ABOUT THE AUTHOR

At a time of life when most people begin to slow down, **Kathy Peach** decided to head for the Southwest to live near her daughter after being in Tennessee her entire life. She then followed her lifelong dreams of earning a college degree and writing a children's book. Peach graduated from Arizona State University with a degree in Early Childhood/Early Childhood Special Education and taught for the Head Start program in Phoenix. In developing *The Tiniest Tumbleweed*, she incorporated a method of writing children's literature whereby readers can believe in a life of limitless possibilities, with theories from a psychologist who taught that all people have the capability to achieve. It is this strategic approach to the creation of *The Tiniest Tumbleweed* that makes Peach's first book not only a delight, but an inspiration.

ABOUT THE ILLUSTRATOR

Alex Lopez is a self-taught artist whose career initially developed in the video game industry and has extended to various other areas in multimedia art production. He currently freelances as an art director which includes building and training artistic teams. Residing in California's Silicon Valley with his wife and identical triplet daughters, Lopez has a strong passion for enhancing his skills as an artist, yet his true joy comes from spending time with his family. In addition to *The Tiniest Tumbleweed*, Lopez has illustrated *Gator, Gator, Second Grader (Classroom Pet... Or Not?)* by Conrad J. Storad and *Three Clever Coyote Pups* by Sharon I. Ritt.